SPIROS
THE GHOST
PHOENIX

With special thanks to Michael Ford

*To three young heroes – Charlie,
Alex and Tom*

www.beastquest.co.uk

ORCHARD BOOKS
338 Euston Road, London NW1 3BH
Orchard Books Australia
Level 17/207 Kent St, Sydney, NSW 2000

A Paperback Original
First published in Great Britain in 2008

A CIP catalogue record for this book is available
from the British Library.

ISBN 978 1 84616 994 6

15 17 19 20 18 16

Printed and bound by CPI Group (UK) Ltd, Croydon, CR0 4YY

The paper and board used in this paperback are natural recyclable
products made from wood grown in sustainable forests. The
manufacturing processes conform to the environmental regulations
of the country of origin.

Orchard Books is a division of Hachette Children's Books,
an Hachette Livre UK company.

www.hachettelivre.co.uk

SPIROS
THE GHOST PHOENIX

BY ADAM BLADE

ORCHARD

THE ICY P.

THE NORTHERN MOUNTAINS

THE C

WESTERN OCEAN

THE FOREST OF FEAR

THE

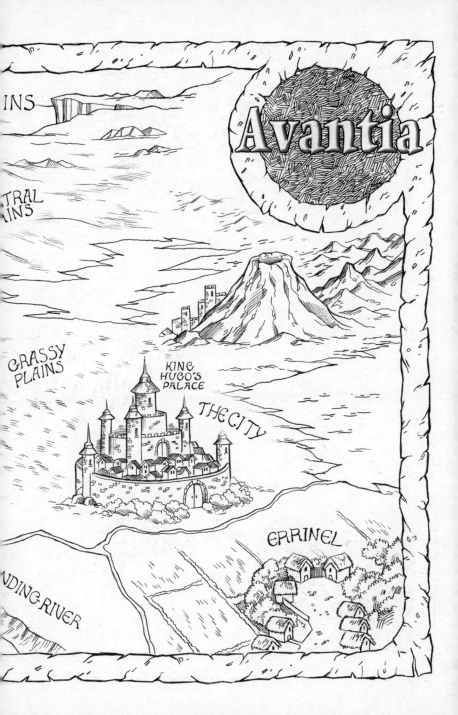

THE GATHERING

*W*elcome to Avantia – its deepest, darkest depths. I am Henry, brother of Taladon the Swift and uncle to Tom, Avantia's brave young hero.

I am also the latest prisoner of Malvel's evil magic. Like a bat in the night, the Dark Wizard swooped and snatched my wife Maria and I from our home in Errinel. Now he holds us captive in an underground prison, beneath a secret location far from any human eye.

It has been a great pleasure to see Tom grow into a heroic young boy. But simply being a hero will not see him through his most difficult Quest yet – saving his family. My nephew will need all his wits and courage just to find us. But first, he must track down a new Beast…one who has been hidden from Avantia for many years.

Can Tom find this elusive Beast and enlist her help in completing his new Quest?

We certainly hope so…our lives depend upon it.

Stay brave.

Henry, Uncle of Tom

CHAPTER ONE

THE EVIL OF MALVEL

"Do you realise where we are, Tom?" said Elenna, as he helped her over a fallen trunk. Silver bounded over to stand beside Tom's stallion, Storm.

Tom peered through the dense trees. It had been raining and the smell of damp leaves filled his nostrils. "In a forest?" he joked.

"This is where we first met!" said Elenna.

Tom thought back. He'd been on a mission to free Ferno the fire dragon from Malvel the Dark Wizard's evil curse. "It was my first Beast Quest," he said. "You were hunting rabbits with Silver."

"That's right," said Elenna, stroking Silver's neck. "The forest doesn't seem as frightening now."

Tom nodded. After all the Beasts they'd faced together, the darkness of the forest no longer made him shiver. He placed his foot in Storm's stirrup and heaved himself up. Elenna climbed into the saddle behind him.

"Once we clear the forest and cross the plains, it's only a short ride to Errinel," said Elenna.

Tom smiled. "I can't wait. It's been

so long since I last saw my aunt and uncle. Something to eat and a soft bed is just what we need after all our adventures."

Silver barked and jumped up on his hind legs.

"And there might even be some bones for you!" laughed Elenna.

Tom steered his stallion across the mossy forest floor. But something was bothering him. He sensed that he and his friends were not alone. He let his hand drop onto the hilt of his sword.

"What's wrong?" Elenna asked.

A sound like a crack of lightning splintered the silence, and a cloud of smoke appeared between the trees. Tom slipped from the saddle, unsheathing his sword and gripping his shield. Silver whimpered and Storm swished his tail.

"Is it Malvel?" whispered Elenna, dismounting.

But as the smoke cleared, a familiar figure emerged. He was wearing a cloak of faded blue and red silk.

"Aduro!" said Elenna, rushing forwards.

Tom put away his sword. But the look in the old man's grey eyes made him anxious. "What is it, Aduro?" he asked.

"I had to come immediately," said the good wizard.

Even Silver stopped leaping about, and Elenna fell back beside Tom.

Aduro stroked his wispy beard. "Tom, Elenna, you must steel yourselves for terrible news," he warned. "Malvel has committed his worst crime yet."

Fear crept over Tom's heart. He felt Elenna's fingers grip his arm.

Aduro looked Tom in the eye. "A messenger arrived at King Hugo's castle this morning with a dreadful tale. Last night a weary traveller came to your village. The local tavern owner thought there was something unusual about him, but your Uncle Henry and Aunt Maria, kind people that they are, gave him a meal and a bed for the night. This morning they were gone. And so was the traveller."

"Perhaps they offered to accompany him to his destination," said Tom.

"I'm afraid not," said Aduro. "The traveller left behind a message…" The wizard pulled out a piece of parchment from his cloak and handed it to Tom.

He unfolded the thin paper and read: "Dear Tom, if I cannot hurt you, I will kill those closest to you. Malvel."

"Oh, Tom!" gasped Elenna.

Tom felt sick. His hand clenched

into a fist around the parchment. "I'll rescue Uncle Henry and Aunt Maria," he vowed. "While there's blood in my veins, I won't rest until I get them back."

CHAPTER TWO

A NEW BEAST

Tom looked at the good wizard.
"Where are they now?" he asked.

Aduro shook his head sadly. "I've
tried everything in my power, but
I can't see where Malvel has
taken them."

Tom felt anger flood through him.
"How dare he? The fight is between
Malvel and me. There was no reason
to involve my family."

"Malvel's heart is dark," said Aduro. "He will hurt you any way he can."

Suddenly a breeze blew through the clearing, rustling the leaves. With it came the sound of a low cackle. Storm reared up in fright.

"Malvel!" said Elenna.

Tom nodded. He'd recognise that laugh anywhere. "There must be some way to find out where they are," he said.

"What about the enchanted map?" suggested Elenna.

Tom dashed over to Storm and unlaced his saddlebag. The magical map of Avantia had helped them locate all the Beasts on their previous Quests. Perhaps it would help them find his aunt and uncle, too.

He knelt on the forest floor and unrolled the parchment. Elenna and Aduro stood over him. But no pulsing green line appeared to show them the way.

"Malvel's evil magic is strong," sighed Aduro. "He has overcome the power of the map."

"But there must be something we can do!" said Elenna.

"There may be one thing," the good wizard muttered. "No, no, it's too dangerous…"

"What?" said Tom. "I'll do anything!"

Aduro placed both hands on Tom's shoulders. "If you want to rescue your aunt and uncle, you will have to undertake your toughest Quest yet. You must face another Beast, the likes of which you have never seen."

"I didn't know there were any others," said Tom.

"I'm talking of a Beast not seen for generations. The lost seventh Beast of Avantia."

Elenna gasped. "A seventh Beast?"

"Yes," said Aduro. "As well as the six good Beasts that patrol Avantia, there was a seventh created to guard the skies. She was born after the others. Let me show you."

The wizard brought his hands together in a loud clap that echoed through the forest, then rubbed his palms. Tom looked on, baffled, and even Storm and Silver stepped closer.

A thin trail of smoke emerged from between Aduro's clasped hands. It rose into the air, forming a cloud. Then, in the middle of the cloud, a shape emerged. It looked like a bird, but its wings were ablaze with a golden flame.

"Is that the Seventh Beast?"
asked Elenna.

"It is," said Aduro. "Her name is
Spiros the phoenix. If anyone can
help you find where Malvel has
taken Tom's aunt and uncle, it is

Spiros. She is blessed with the power of All-Sight – magic that even I do not possess. It allows her to see into the far reaches of Avantia and beyond. Nothing is hidden from her."

The cloud of smoke evaporated into the forest, and with it disappeared the image of the phoenix.

"Where can we find her?" Tom wondered.

Aduro frowned. "I wish it were that easy," he said. "But Spiros hasn't been seen in the skies of Avantia for many years. No one knows where she is."

"How can that be?" asked Elenna.

"It was Malvel," said Aduro, his face darkening. "Before he bewitched the first six good Beasts, he cast a spell over Spiros."

"What did he do to her?" Tom asked.

"He separated her body from her spirit," said the wizard.

Tom was confused. "How is that possible?" he asked. "Is she dead?"

"Not quite dead," said Aduro. "But halfway there. Spiros is a ghost!"

Elenna drew a sharp breath.
A ghost phoenix!

"If you challenge Malvel again," said Aduro, "you will need all your bravery and wits to survive. It will be your most dangerous Quest yet."

But Tom had already made his decision. His aunt and uncle were his only family. He had to go. He looked at Elenna. She was pale, but gave a defiant nod. It was settled then.

"We are ready," said Tom.

Aduro smiled. "I knew your courage would not fail. Now I must leave."

There was a flash near the wizard's feet that made Tom and Elenna step back. A curtain of smoke rose up, concealing him. When it disappeared, Aduro no longer stood before them.

"He's gone!" said Elenna.

"Come on," Tom said. "We need to track down Spiros. Let's get out of the forest." He led Elenna quickly through the trees, with Silver and Storm right behind them.

"But how are we going to find her?" asked Elenna. "She could be anywhere in Avantia. It might take years!"

Elenna was right. Even riding Storm at full gallop, there was no telling how long their search would take them.

Tom took out the map again. It showed the whole kingdom, as far as the icy plains in the north. "There must be a way!" he said. Then his eyes rested on the mountain where Ferno the fire dragon lived. It gave him an idea. "Wait, what if we asked…"

"...the good Beasts!" Elenna
finished.

"Yes!" said Tom. "Avantia's too big
for us to search quickly on our own,
but with the help of the Beasts it
might be possible."

"Which one shall we call first?"
asked Elenna.

Tom pondered for a moment.
"Ferno's mountain is close by. If this
ghost phoenix patrols the skies,
Ferno can help us search there.
Perhaps the other Beasts will be able
to help, too."

Tom rubbed the dragon's scale in
his shield. But nothing stirred in the
silence of the forest.

"Try again," said Elenna. "The
Beasts won't let you down."

Tom did as she said, but not even
a bird rustled in the branches.

Just as he was about to give up, a
screech filled their ears and ashes
fluttered down around their feet.
A shadow drifted above the trees.

"It's Ferno!" said Tom.

CHAPTER THREE

THE GOOD DRAGON

Ferno circled above the trees, his jagged black wings blotting out the sun. Tom remembered how terrified he had been the first time he saw the colossal creature's blood-red eyes, but now he was filled with pride.

Ferno dived, opening his scaly wings to slow his descent. He landed gracefully in the clearing and strode

towards them, his claws flattening
the grass and his thick tail dragging
across the ground. He towered above
them, as tall as ten houses.

"Thank you for helping us!"
shouted Tom.

Ferno lifted his head and blew out
a stream of fire, filling the air with
the bitter smell of sulphur. Storm
whinnied a greeting.

The Beast folded his legs and lay on his stomach, leaving one wing extended towards them.

"He wants us to climb up," Tom said to Elenna.

"What about Storm and Silver?" she asked.

"There's room for them as well," said Tom as he scrambled onto Ferno's wing. The scales felt hard and slippery beneath his hands. Elenna led Storm and Silver, and soon they were settled in the hollow between the dragon's shoulders. Ferno rose to his feet and opened his huge wings.

"Hold on tight!" Tom said.

Ferno charged through the clearing. The trees on the far side approached quickly, but the Beast showed no signs of slowing. Just when it seemed they would smash into the trees, Ferno launched himself into the air. Tom whooped as the treetops fell away below them. The day was beautifully clear and he could see for miles. To the south, King's Hugo's palace stood over the great city. Beyond that was Tom's home village of Errinel. Avantia looked so beautiful underneath them. It was difficult to think that Malvel's evil was once again at work.

"We need to find Spiros!" shouted Tom to Ferno. "We must search the skies."

The fire dragon seemed to understand, and flew up beyond the clouds, circling in wide arcs. They searched until the sun reached its highest point, then headed north. The temperature began to drop. Tom scanned the sky for any sign of

the ghost phoenix, but he could
see nothing apart from the
occasional eagle.

Soon Ferno's wings were beating
with less energy.

"It's too cold," said Elenna. "And
Ferno's tired."

Tom patted the fire dragon's neck.
"You've done enough, friend."

Ferno snorted and wheeled in the air, taking them back towards the grassy plains. A herd of cattle was grazing on the long grass. The creatures scattered, letting out startled moos, as the mighty dragon dropped out of the sky and came to a stop.

Tom, Elenna, Storm and Silver climbed down from Ferno's back, while the great Beast stood patiently.

"Thanks, old friend," said Tom. "You can go back to your mountain now."

With a farewell roar, the fire dragon took to the skies again.

Watching him fly away, Tom felt deflated. The golden chainmail he had won in his last Quest was meant to give him strength of heart, but right now it didn't feel like it was working. How would he ever find his aunt and uncle?

"We have to widen our search if we're going to find Spiros," he said. "What about the plains?"

"But they're vast," said Elenna. "Storm is strong, but even he can't cover that much ground."

"I know a Beast who can!" said Tom, and rubbed the fragment of horseshoe embedded in his shield.

After a few moments, the cattle began to crowd together.

"Something's spooked them," said Elenna.

Beneath Tom's feet, the ground quaked. The cows suddenly split into two groups, and a path opened up between them. A shape appeared on the horizon.

"Tagus!" Tom shouted. The soft rumble of hooves became louder as the horse-man galloped towards

them. With the body of a stallion but
the torso of a man, he towered over
Storm. Shaggy black hair grew in a
tangled mess on his head. He slowed
in front of Tom and Elenna, his chest
heaving as he pawed the ground.

"Welcome, Tagus," said Tom. "We

have to find Spiros the ghost
phoenix. Can you help us?"

Tagus couldn't speak but he seemed
to understand, and lowered himself
to his knees so that Tom and Elenna
could climb onto his back.

"Storm and Silver can stay here,"
Tom said as they mounted. "We'll
have to go alone."

Storm was grazing contentedly and
Silver was already darting off into the
long grass. Tom gripped the Beast's
waist and they set off at a canter over
the plains.

Soon they were galloping through
the grass at incredible speed. The
feeling of power beneath Tom was
immense. It was impossible to speak
over the thunder of Tagus's hooves,
but he felt Elenna's fingers digging
into his sides.

Tom scoured the grasslands for signs of Spiros, and was beginning to give up hope when he heard a wailing sound from behind a hillock. Tagus slowed to a trot. Could it be the ghost phoenix?

"That way!" shouted Tom. Tagus set off up the incline. As they neared the top a howl pierced Tom's ears, followed by a low growl. A flash of brown appeared to their right. But it wasn't Spiros.

"Hyenas!" cried Elenna, placing an arrow to her bow.

Another creature skulked to their left, lifting its nose to sniff the air. Tagus swivelled on his hooves as Tom counted ten hyenas fanning out around them. He knew they wouldn't normally attack a Beast the size of Tagus, but weighed down with

two humans, he must have seemed
an easier target.

One of the ugly animals darted at
Tagus's leg, and received a kick that
sent it sprawling. Another followed,
but Elenna fired an arrow, and with
a yelp the hyena limped away.

"Good work," said Tom, then

turned to see a large hyena bounding towards them. It leaped through the air, jaws slavering. There was no time to draw his sword, so he smashed his shield into the hyena's head. The creature fell to the ground, then dragged itself away, followed by the rest of the pack.

"That was close," said Elenna.

"Let's get away from here and keep searching," said Tom.

He steered the horse-man towards the highest part of the plains, a plateau scattered with giant rocks. When they arrived at the top, Tom slipped from the Beast's back, and clambered up one of the largest boulders, staring out across the great plains.

His golden helmet had given him the power of enhanced vision. He had won it on his Quest against Zepha the monster squid and it was now safely locked away in King Hugo's castle. He trained his eyes on every corner of the plains, desperately looking for a sign of the ghost phoenix.

"Anything?" Elenna asked.

Tom shook his head. "Nothing. And I'm not even sure I'll be able to recognise Spiros, since she's a ghost." Tagus stood, waiting for further commands. Tom turned to him. "Thank you, but you should go back to protecting your cattle."

Rearing onto his hind legs, Tagus roared then galloped away, leaving Tom and Elenna alone.

"What now?" asked Elenna.

Tom smiled. "I have one more idea," he said. "Perhaps to find a phoenix, we need to use a phoenix."

"You don't mean..." began Elenna.

"That's right," said Tom. "We need Epos!"

CHAPTER FOUR

SEARCHING THE KINGDOM

Tom took his shield and rubbed the talon of the flame bird that was embedded there.

Almost immediately, a screech cut through the air and a glow appeared on the horizon.

"There she is!" cried Elenna.

The glow grew into the shape of a winged creature. Tom felt his heart fill with joy. Epos's dark red feathers glittered in the sunlight and flames trailed from the tips of her wings. She landed beside them, her talons clattering on the rocks.

Tom placed his foot on Epos's wing and climbed up, settling into the thick feathers at the base of her neck. Elenna sat behind him.

Epos took to the air once more, gliding low over the plains. Then she flapped her wings and climbed higher.

"Keep your eyes open for Spiros," Tom said to Elenna.

He searched the sky for a flash of golden flame, but there was nothing. Tom steered Epos east, towards the volcano that was her home, but there was no sign of the seventh Beast there, either.

"Spiros!" he cried out in desperation. "Where are you?"

With a heavy heart, he guided the flame bird back to the plains where Storm and Silver were waiting.

As they jumped down from Epos's back, Silver dashed forwards and placed his paws on Elenna's chest, licking her face. Storm nuzzled Tom's hair.

"It's good to see you, too, boy," Tom said.

Epos took to the skies again, circled once, then gave a caw of farewell. Tom and Elenna waved goodbye.

"I think we need to try the northern mountains next," Tom said.

"Won't it be too cold for a phoenix there?" asked Elenna.

"Too cold for a living phoenix, perhaps," replied Tom. "But not a ghost phoenix."

Mounting Storm, they galloped across the plains towards the foothills of the mountains. The sun started to dip in the sky and the snow-capped mountains towered above them. If Tom could get up there, among the highest peaks of Avantia, he would be able to see the entire kingdom.

They ascended the mountain path,
climbing towards a pass that ran
between two enormous peaks. Tom
took out the last of their supplies
from Storm's saddlebag – two Ruby
Guya fruits from the heart of the
Dark Jungle. The juice dripped down
his chin as he ate, and it gave him
just the boost of energy he needed.

Soon the air cooled and the path became difficult as they skirted the edge of the slope. Silver placed his paws carefully among the loose rocks, but Storm kept stumbling. Finally, as they reached an overhanging section of cliff, Tom drew up the reins.

"We can't go any further on horseback," he said. "It's too dangerous. Storm and Silver should shelter here. We need a guide."

"Arcta?" asked Elenna.

Tom nodded. He rubbed the eagle's feather token in his shield.

Silver lifted his nose into the air.

"What is it, boy?" asked Elenna.

A low rumbling echoed around them. Storm whinnied and took a few jittery steps backwards. From a ridge opposite, a section of rocks

crumbled and crashed down into
the valley.

"Is it a landslide?" asked Elenna.

Before Tom could answer, a huge
hairy hand appeared over the edge
of the cliff ahead. Its claws were
yellow and as thick as wooden
planks. Arcta the mountain giant
heaved himself over the precipice
and stood before them.

Each of the Beast's legs was as thick as a tree trunk, and his muscular arms looked as if they could smash buildings to pieces. When Arcta saw Tom and Elenna, he let out a roar, and his face split into a wide grin, revealing brown, crooked teeth. His single eye twinkled with kindness.

Tom pointed to the highest mountains. "We need to go up there," he shouted. "Can you take us?"

Arcta turned his massive head in the direction of the snowy peaks, then scooped Tom up with one hand. With the other he grabbed Elenna. She let out a little squeal, which turned into a laugh. The Beast was gentle, and the pads of his palms were as soft and warm as worn leather.

Leaving Storm and Silver beneath the overhang, Arcta carried Tom and Elenna higher into the peaks. Rocks scattered from his giant feet. At one point a line of trees blocked their route, but Arcta pushed them aside, bending the trunks like twigs. As they passed through, the trees sprung upright again, showering the ground with leaves.

Soon they reached the snow. Tom peered over the top of the giant's

warm fist to look out for signs of
Spiros. They checked behind huge
boulders and in shallow gorges. As
the snow became deeper, Arcta's feet
left indentations as long and wide as
market carts. But there was no sign
of life among the snow.

The mountain giant set Tom
and Elenna down carefully for a
moment's rest. Tom immediately
scanned the horizon with his magical
sight. There was nothing to see but
the lonely jagged peaks.

Fresh flakes of snow had started to
fall. Tom shivered. He wondered if
Malvel had sent a snowstorm to
frustrate him. He was worried that he
had used four Beasts' help already,
yet was no closer to finding Spiros.
Malvel was winning.

Tom let out a yell of frustration that echoed across the mountain range. Without Spiros and the gift of All-Sight, he would never be able to rescue his aunt and uncle from Malvel's clutches.

"I've failed," he muttered.

Then he felt Elenna's hand on his shoulder.

"This isn't over," she said. "We mustn't give up the search."

"Where else is there to look?" said Tom. "I've asked almost all of the good Beasts for help, and we still can't find Spiros."

Elenna's face lit up.

"What is it?" Tom asked.

"I do have one idea," she replied. "Didn't Aduro tell us that Spiros was born after the other six Beasts, in order to patrol the skies?"

"I think so, yes. Why is that important?"

"Don't you see?" said Elenna. "She was the seventh Beast to arrive. Perhaps if we get all six Beasts together, in one place…"

Tom stood up and gripped Elenna by the shoulders. "Spiros will return!" he said. "Yes! Of course. Six came before her, now six must come again!"

CHAPTER FIVE

SUMMONING THE GHOST PHOENIX

The sky had darkened. Looking to the west, Tom could see that the sun was nearing the horizon. It was snowing heavily now, and the icy flakes tickled his face.

"It'll be night soon," he said. "We have to get back down to Storm and Silver."

Arcta scooped them up once more.

Tom felt exhilarated as the Beast ran down the mountain in bounding strides. If their new plan worked, they'd find Spiros and save his aunt and uncle from Malvel.

Once they were near the foothills, they said goodbye to Arcta.

"We know the way from here," said Tom. "But we may need you again soon."

The mountain giant grunted, then trudged off through the snow. Tom and Elenna slid down the rest of the slope on their behinds, whooping with delight. Storm and Silver were waiting where they'd left them, sheltered under the rocks.

Tom took blankets from Storm's saddlebag. He gave one to Elenna and wrapped the other around his shoulders. Silver and Storm had their thick coats to keep them warm. Then Tom led his three companions to the base of the mountains by the light of the moon, which glowed faintly behind thin veils of mist.

"We need to get to the Western Ocean by dawn," he said. "We have to find Sepron, then summon the other Beasts there. I'm afraid we won't be able to rest tonight."

"I feel more awake than ever," said Elenna. "And so does Silver, by the look of him."

Her wolf was alert, with his ears pricked and his tail up.

Tom patted Storm's flank. "I think Storm will be able to keep going, too."

The stallion snorted and bucked his hind legs.

With Tom and Elenna on his back, Storm charged into the night. Tom could hear Elenna's teeth chattering behind him, but she didn't complain. The stars flickered above as bats swooped around them.

It was a cold dawn when they reached the Western Ocean, but

Tom's blood felt warm. The sea
was calm, with only light ripples
disturbing the surface.

Storm stopped on the pebbled
shoreline and Silver ran ahead to

splash in the shallows. Tom knew
what he had to do. He pulled his
shield off his shoulder and put his
hand into the strap. The serpent's
tooth would draw Sepron to him.

Tom rubbed his sleeve against the
tooth, then held the shield so it faced
out towards the sea.

A wave travelled along the water, crashing onto the beach. Silver scurried away from the shore.

"There's something out there," said Elenna.

A larger wave, almost as high as Tom's thighs, came in with the swell. Then, a hundred paces offshore, something broke the surface – a flash of colours like a rainbow.

"It's Sepron!" whispered Tom. The multicoloured scales appeared again, this time fifty paces out. The sea serpent was swimming towards them.

Sepron's head reared out of the shallows and rose up on a slender green neck. He opened his mouth to reveal curved fangs. Slimy seaweed was tangled in his gaping jaws. But Tom knew that despite his terrifying appearance, Sepron was a good Beast.

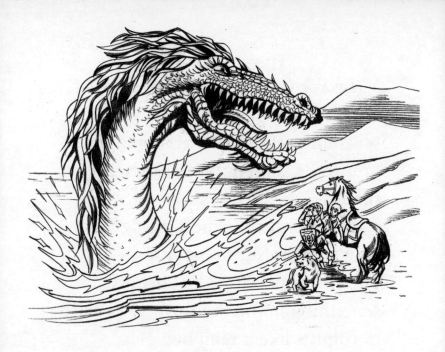

The serpent crashed into the water
again, sending up a wall of spray
that soaked Tom and Elenna. Tom
couldn't help laughing, and Elenna
burst into giggles.

"It's time to put your theory to the
test," said Tom. Turning to face
the mainland, he held up his shield,
sending out his summons to the
other five Beasts. "Good Beasts of
Avantia. Unite!"

The wood began to shake on his arm. As the shield vibrated, Tom forced himself to continue holding it out. All the magical symbols – the scale, the tooth, the feather, the horse-shoe, the bell and the talon – glowed in the dawn light. His shoulder screamed with pain, but he gritted his teeth. It was the most powerful sorcery Tom had ever experienced. *I have to go through with it*, he thought.

"Tom, look!" shouted Elenna. "The Beasts are coming!"

Tom lowered his shield. His heart almost stopped at the sight. Standing at the edge of the beach were the other five Beasts. Arcta stood beside Tagus, whose dark hair was wet with pearls of dew. Ferno stood at one end of the row and blew a spurt of fire, while Epos hovered at the other end, her flaming feathers adding light to the gloomy morning. Finally, Nanook stepped forwards, her shaggy white fur grubby after travelling so far from the icy plains.

"They're all here!" said Tom happily.

Arcta plucked both Elenna and Tom from the ground, placing them on his

shoulders, and Tom at once looked inland for any sign of Spiros. The mist was beginning to lift now, and as time passed, the sun's light grew stronger. What if they were wrong? What if Spiros couldn't be tempted to come to them?

"Now what?" said Elenna, but almost as soon as she had spoken the words, Ferno thumped the pebbles with his tail. Nanook roared and Arcta bellowed. Tagus reared on his hind legs and stamped the ground. Epos lifted her beak and gave a deafening screech. Finally, Sepron splashed in the water, sending up huge waves. Soon the cries of all six Beasts echoed across the dawn, making Tom's skin tingle.

"They're calling for Spiros," he shouted over the din.

A screech penetrated the mist. Tom turned on Arcta's shoulders. The Beasts twisted their mighty heads to look. Silver was barking excitedly and Storm whinnied, pacing up and down on the shore.

"Look!" said Elenna, pointing.

Tom peered to a spot in the sky. It looked at first as though the stars were still out – a patch of the sky sparkled even though it was daytime.

Then a shape, no more than a shadow, appeared above the mist. It moved quickly, soaring towards them. Tom wasn't afraid. This is what he'd been waiting for. Spiros the ghost phoenix was coming!

CHAPTER SIX

JOURNEY ABOVE THE CLOUDS

Spiros soared across the sky, weaving in and out of the clouds. The red feathers of her body shone like polished rubies, but her wings were golden. Her eyes were emerald green and she was surrounded by a luminous mist.

"She's beautiful!" gasped Elenna.

Tom tapped Arcta's shoulder and

the Beast lowered him and Elenna to the ground. Tom called up to Spiros. "I have to find where Malvel has taken my aunt and uncle!"

Spiros twisted her wings and hovered in the air above them.

"I think she wants us to go with her," said Tom.

"But we can't ride a ghost phoenix!" Elenna said. "We'd fall right through."

"But we can follow one!" said Tom.

"Of course!" cried Elenna, and together they dashed towards Epos and climbed up onto her back. Storm trotted forwards and lowered his head. Tom could tell his brave stallion was sad to be saying goodbye to his master again. Silver appeared at Storm's side and gave a high-pitched whine.

"We'll be back soon!" said Tom.

"But this part of the Quest is too dangerous for you two."

Ferno extended a giant wing over the two animals.

"He'll look after them," said Elenna. "Goodbye, Silver. Goodbye, Storm!"

Epos left the ground with a flap of her wings, and the other Beasts grew small as the flame bird broke through the layer of cloud into the clear blue sky. Spiros turned and flew north, her spectre-like form gliding through the air like a wisp of coloured cloud.

Epos set off in pursuit, her flaming wings beating the air.

"Where do you think Spiros is taking us?" asked Elenna.

"I don't know," said Tom, pulling his silver compass from his pocket. The needle wavered, before pointing towards *Destiny*. But as they watched,

it suddenly swung around – and
signalled *Danger*.

"It can't be both," said Elenna. She
gasped as the needle swung back to
Destiny again.

"Perhaps it can," said Tom, putting

the instrument away. "We have no choice. We have to trust Spiros and her gift of All-Sight."

They soared ahead, flying among the tallest of the mountain peaks that broke through the cloud. Despite the wind whistling past their ears and flattening their clothes against their bodies, everything was eerily calm. Spiros's golden wings, shifting in and out of focus, glinted in the sunlight.

"We must be travelling to the icy plains – Nanook's kingdom," Tom said.

"But nothing can live there," said Elenna. "It's too cold."

Tom knew she was right. If his aunt and uncle had been taken there, perhaps he was too late. But he couldn't give up hope. Aduro had told him that Spiros could help, and he wasn't about to lose faith now.

They left the mountains behind.
Although the sky ahead was clear,
something didn't feel right.

"Elenna," he whispered, "I don't
think we're alone."

"I know," she said with a shiver.
"I feel it, too."

Suddenly, a shriek filled Tom's
ears, and they were cast in shadow.
Tom and Elenna swivelled round.
There was another phoenix! It was
the same size and shape as Spiros,
but its feathers were black and it
smelled of rotting flesh. Instead of
scattering radiant light, it rained
sulphurous, hot ash. Its talons looked
as if they were made of charred iron.

"It's disgusting!" said Elenna.

The black phoenix dipped a wing
and swooped towards them.

"Hold on!" Tom shouted, and
leaned forwards, tugging at Epos's
feathers. The flame bird rolled to one
side and the black phoenix's talons
brushed past Tom's shoulder.

Epos continued to roll, and for
a moment Tom felt completely
weightless as the world turned upside
down. Elenna cried out behind him,
her arms tightening around his
middle. Then Epos turned full circle
and righted herself.

Tom saw that the material of his
tunic was torn at the top of his arm.
Any closer, and the black phoenix's
talons would have taken off his head.

But as the black phoenix climbed
again, Tom saw something else.
Riding on the evil creature's back
was a girl with a pale face. Her long
dark hair flowed in the wind and she
stared at Tom with coal-black eyes.

"Who is that?" shouted Elenna.

Tom didn't have time to answer.
The girl was already drawing
her sword.

CHAPTER SEVEN

DUEL IN
THE SKIES

The black phoenix closed in on them
again, and Tom just had time to draw
his own sword as the girl brought
hers down. He parried the blow, but
the force nearly knocked him off
Epos's back.

The black phoenix climbed high
above them, preparing for another
attack. Spiros remained at a safe

distance. Tom knew there was nothing the ghost phoenix could do.

"That girl must be one of Malvel's agents!" said Elenna.

"Keep low," said Tom, raising his sword as the girl guided her phoenix towards them again.

"Attack!" she screamed.

As it swooped down, the black phoenix plunged its talons into Epos's side. The flame bird let out a pained cry as a clump of her feathers was torn away. Tom felt Elenna's hands loosen on his waist.

"Help!" she screamed. Tom twisted around to see that Elenna had slipped off Epos's back and was clinging desperately to the fire bird's wing. Keeping a firm grip on Epos's neck feathers with one hand, Tom sheathed his sword and reached down with his free arm.

"Grab my hand!" he shouted.

Elenna's face was pale with fear
and her knuckles were white. "I can't
let go," she yelled back. "I'll fall!"

Tom reached down, feeling the
sinews in his arm stretch. Just a
little further and he'd be able to
reach his friend…

Then a thud hit him. Epos screeched. The girl's black phoenix was attacking again. Tom felt the flame bird tip to one side, and it was all he could do to hang on. Spiros was above them now, squawking desperately. Elenna lost her grip. Her fingers slipped through Epos's feathers and she cried out in terror as she plummeted through the sky. Then the sounds of her screams were lost as she disappeared into the mist.

"No!" yelled Tom. He took off his shield and threw it after her with all his might. "Elenna," he shouted. "Use my shield!" There was a chance that its magic would stop her falling – if she could catch it. Tom steered Epos down into the clouds after Elenna, but the black phoenix blocked his path. The pale-faced girl let out a cackle.

"You'll pay for what you've done," Tom shouted, his anger swelling.

"We'll see about that," replied the girl. There was something familiar about her face – but Tom had no time to think about where he might have seen her before. The girl was flying towards him again.

This time Tom was ready. Their swords met with a clang that sent a shock wave down Tom's arm. He swung a blow at her, but she ducked out of the way, as quick as lightning. Epos locked talons with the black phoenix, her sharp beak darting at the evil creature's throat. The air was filled with feathers. Tom saw that Spiros was circling them – but with no real body, there was nothing the ghost phoenix could do to help.

The girl stabbed at Tom, and he locked the blade of her sword with his hilt, grabbed her arm and pulled her towards him. He held his own blade at her throat, leaning as far from Epos as he dared.

"You've lost," said Tom. "You can't defeat me."

She struggled, but he gripped her sword arm even more tightly.

"Tell me who you are," he said in her ear.

The girl stopped struggling and

smiled cruelly. "Look closely," she hissed. "Surely I remind you of someone. My name is Sethrina."

Now it was clear to Tom. This was the sister of Seth, the evil boy Tom had encountered on a previous Beast Quest.

"You work for Malvel!" he said.

"One day everyone will work for Malvel," Sethrina replied.

"Never!" shouted Tom. "While there's blood in my veins, I'll keep Avantia free. Run back to your master and tell him I said that."

Tom released Sethrina's arm; he had to go after Elenna. But immediately Sethrina lunged with her sword. Tom blocked her strike easily.

"Don't you know when to give up?" he shouted. "You can't win, and if you're not careful it's your phoenix that will get killed."

Sethrina smiled wickedly. "Oh, Tom, you don't want to kill my phoenix, believe me. That would be very bad for your precious Avantia..."

There was a screech and Tom looked up to see Spiros hovering in the air above. Suddenly, he saw that Spiros and the black phoenix were exactly the same size, with identical beaks and talons. Beneath the black phoenix's layer of grime, Tom could just make out the same red scales as... Then the awful realisation hit him: the black phoenix had taken over Spiros's body!

Sethrina was watching his face closely. "Ah, you've understood!" She patted her phoenix's neck. "Meet Nawdren."

"That body belongs to Spiros!" shouted Tom.

"Ha!" laughed Sethrina. "Nawdren has nothing to do with Spiros. Or, at least, she never will again!"

Then she lunged at Tom with her sword.

He dodged the blow and aimed his own sword at Nawdren's beak. If he could distract the evil phoenix, it

would at least give him time to help
Elenna. He hit the beak with the flat
of his sword, as hard as he could. The
phoenix drew her head back and
screeched in agony, wheeling away
through the clouds. Tom heard
Sethrina's cry of anger as she was
carried away.

Immediately he steered Epos in a
steep dive down through the clouds.
"I'm coming, Elenna!" he called
out, but dread filled his heart. What
was waiting for him on the icy plains
of Avantia? If his friend was dead,
would he ever be able to complete
this Beast Quest alone?

REBIRTH

Welcome back to Avantia, my friends. You can see that my nephew has done well so far, but his Quest to save his family is far from over. The Dark Wizard Malvel always has an extra trick up his sleeve.

A new Beast, controlled by a new foe. This Quest has just gone from dangerous to deadly.

Tom and Elenna have achieved the impossible in summoning the great ghost phoenix, Spiros, and now Tom must find his family. But Malvel will stop at nothing to keep us apart forever.

Join us in wishing Avantia's young heroes well.

We're depending on them like never before.

Stay brave.

Henry, Uncle of Tom

CHAPTER ONE

THE LAND OF ICE

The land of the icy plains was white with patches of blue where the ice was thin. The bitter wind had carved icebergs into strange shapes. Spiros flew beside Tom and Epos.

"We have to find Elenna!" Tom shouted.

The flame bird headed down to the ice-shelf, her massive shadow rippling over the land below.

Suddenly, Spiros squawked and dropped away. Tom could see where she was making for – a patch of brown lying in the middle of a frozen lake. Elenna! As he guided Epos to follow, he saw his shield on the ice a few paces away from his friend.

Epos landed on the frozen surface, her talons sending up shards of ice.

Spiros floated to the ground without a sound. Tom leaped off the flame bird's back and rushed to Elenna. The ice creaked beneath his feet. Beside her body was a hole in the ice, and Tom could see the water below, lapping at the edges. He kneeled down next to his friend. Her clothes were soaking wet. He didn't understand: had she fallen through the ice and then pulled herself out of the freezing water? Surely that was impossible. He saw her lips were turning blue. Ice crystals, like tiny jewels, had already begun to form on her eyelashes.

"Elenna!" he whispered, then put his head on her soaking chest and listened. She still had a heartbeat. Placing his hand by her open mouth, he felt the slight warmth of shallow, regular breathing.

She was alive!

"Elenna, it's me, Tom," he said, shaking her shoulder a little.

Her eyelids fluttered, then she opened her eyes. "Tom?"

"Can you get up?" he asked.

Elenna sat up carefully, then let out a deep shiver. "I...I'm so cold," she stammered.

Tom knew that if Elenna didn't get warm soon, she would die. He lifted her onto his back and carried her to the edge of the frozen lake. In the shelter of a tall ice-stack, they sat down in the snow. Epos hopped over to them, extending a wing which burst into low, gentle flames, bathing Elenna in heat. Not for the first time, Tom was thankful to have the good Beasts of Avantia on his side.

When Elenna had stopped shaking,
Tom asked, "What happened? Did
you catch my shield?"

"Yes," said Elenna. "When I fell,
I thought I was dead for sure. But
then the shield came hurtling towards
me and I heard your voice. As soon
as I caught it, the magic of Arcta's
feather helped me to slow down."

"But the hole in the ice?" Tom asked.

"Well, I was so close to the ground, and travelling so fast, that the shield couldn't save me completely. I saw the lake coming towards me. Then I shut my eyes. That's the last thing I remember. I must have smashed right through the ice."

"But how could you have come up again?" said Tom in bewilderment.

"I don't know…" said Elenna.

Then a huge roar burst from behind the ice-stack, dislodging a layer of snow, which fell in a fine powder around their heads. There was a series of crunching sounds, as though something large was padding towards them, and Spiros let out a soft call. Nanook stood proudly before them.

"She must have plucked me out of

the water," said Elenna. "She saved
my life! Thank you, Nanook."

The giant snow monster of the icy
plains bellowed, ruffling their hair
with the force of her roar. Then she
turned and strode away into the
snow. As she disappeared, a sudden

flash in the sky made them look up. Spiros hovered above them, beating her golden wings.

"We have to get going," said Tom. "If we wait here for too long, Sethrina will find us."

"Sethrina?" asked Elenna.

Tom explained what he had learned about Seth's sister and Nawdren.

"So Nawdren is Spiros's body, separated from Spiros's spirit to carry out Malvel's evil!" Elenna exclaimed, getting to her feet. But as she did so she winced and let out a small cry. "My ankle!" Tom looked down at the bottom of Elenna's leg. Her ankle was red and swollen. "I think it's broken! My body was so cold that I didn't even realise until just now!" she said in despair, sitting back down in the snow.

"Don't worry," said Tom. "Epos's talon can help." He slid back across the ice and retrieved his shield. At Elenna's side, he detached the talon. Its magical healing powers had already helped him on previous Quests. Tom held it to her ankle. The talon warmed in his hand.

"It's working!" said Elenna.

Tom stared at her ankle. Slowly, the swelling disappeared and the redness faded to Elenna's normal skin colour.

"Try standing on it," Tom suggested.

Elenna pushed herself to her feet and gingerly put her weight onto the injured leg. A smile broke out across her face. "It's much better!" she cried out.

They scrambled onto Epos's back, and the flame bird shook the loose snow from her talons. Spiros flapped her wings, rising high above them.

"It looks as if she's ready to go, too!" said Elenna.

"We'll have to be careful," said Tom, as Epos took to the sky. "I have a feeling that we haven't seen the last of Sethrina."

But as they followed Spiros, Tom felt ready for anything Malvel could throw at him. It was time to rescue Uncle Henry and Aunt Maria!

CHAPTER TWO

THE UNDERWORLD

Gusts battered Tom and Elenna as
they clung to Epos's feathers, and
Tom had to brush the snow and ice
crystals from his face to see properly.
Spiros was flying through the sky at
amazing speed and Epos was working
hard to keep up. Snowflakes sizzled
as they hit the flames along her
wings.

"I don't know how Spiros can find her way in these conditions," said Elenna.

"It's the magic of her All-Sight that's guiding her," replied Tom.

Spiros squawked urgently and turned in the air, her wings glowing.

"She's trying to tell us something," said Elenna.

The ghost phoenix suddenly twisted her glittering wings and began to descend. Epos cut through the wind in pursuit.

"This is it!" shouted Tom, as the air streamed around him. "She's found my aunt and uncle!"

They flew down more steeply, picking up speed all the time. Tom could feel the force of the wind rippling his cheeks. Through an eddying swirl of snow, he saw the ice fields on the ground. They were heading straight for them. He felt Elenna tense as she held on to him.

Epos drew in her wings. Her body was almost vertical as it shot to earth.

"Tom, we're going to crash!" shouted Elenna.

"We have to trust Spiros," said Tom, gritting his teeth.

The phoenix didn't pull up. It looked as though her ghostly outline would smash to pieces against the ice, but she slid through the frozen layer without a sound.

Tom fought the urge to pull with all his might on Epos's feathers. "I've put my faith in Spiros until now," he shouted. "While there's blood in my veins, we'll follow her to the end."

The snowy ground rushed towards them. Epos stretched out her talons. A spark appeared between her feet, which grew into a ball of flame, burning almost white with heat.

Epos hurled the fireball at the spot where Spiros had disappeared. It smashed into the frozen wasteland, showering sparks. Then the ice was gone, replaced by a crater. In the middle of the hole, the fireball sank into a patch of boiling sea. They dived into the chasm.

We'll drown! Tom thought. But the

fireball bored a tunnel straight down through the water. Elenna cried out in surprise and Tom gasped. Epos plunged after her fireball as the sea closed in behind them. Tom and Elenna were in a tunnel of air created by Epos, deep below the ocean. They quickly reached the sea floor.

Limp weeds lay flat on the sand and a crab scuttled for shelter beneath a rock covered in bright yellow tendrils. The fireball had spread out around them like a dome, holding back the water. Tom felt the spray dry on his face as the flames warmed him. It was as though they were in another world. Elenna was staring around, her mouth open in wonder.

"This is powerful magic!" said Tom.

"Who would have thought?" Elenna said, stroking Epos's feathers. "A bird at the bottom of the sea!"

The light dimmed and the dome of flame above their heads inched closer. Epos let out a warning squawk.

"Hurry, Tom," said Elenna. "The magic is fading!"

Tom climbed off Epos's back and the

flame bird hopped aside, revealing
something on the sea floor. Tom bent
to inspect it.

"Look, Elenna!" he said. "It's
a trapdoor!"

"Where can it lead?" asked Elenna.

The walls of seawater were closing in again, and the fireball burned less fiercely around them.

"There's only one way to find out," said Tom.

He seized the chain and yanked on it. The trapdoor didn't move.

"Try again," said Elenna. "You can do it."

Tom thought of his golden breastplate. Its magic gave him extra strength. Still, it might not be enough.

He looped the chain around his waist and clenched his fists around one of the links. He took a huge breath, dug his heels into the wet sand, and pushed with every muscle in his legs. The trapdoor moved a finger's width. Tom didn't stop. His kneecaps felt as if they were about to burst open, and his heart was racing, but still he pulled. The trapdoor finally lifted open.

"Quick! Jump in," Tom shouted to Elenna and Epos. The good Beast plunged into the tunnel, with Elenna on her back. The seawater was splashing Tom's hair now. Taking the strain on his arms, he pulled himself along the rope towards the open crack. The protective fire around him was almost out. When he was close to the open trapdoor, he let the coiled chain fall around his feet and jumped down. The door crashed shut behind him and he heard water rushing to fill the space where they had just been standing. They'd made it!

Tom realised he was lying on cold, wet rock. It was pitch-black. He couldn't even see his hand in front of his face.

"Tom?" Elenna's voice echoed around them.

"I'm here!" he said, picking himself up and stumbling through the darkness. His hand closed around Elenna's wrist.

"What now?" she asked.

"We need light," said Tom.

The shape of two wings appeared ahead of them, doused in flame. Epos! As the fire grew, their surroundings became clear. Tom stared about him in astonishment.

"What is this place?" gasped Elenna.

"It must be an underworld!" Tom replied.

CHAPTER THREE

THE CAVERNS OF DANGER

They were standing in a small recess at the edge of a massive cavern. Huge stalactites descended from the cave roof and great pillars of rock grew from the floor, where pools of sticky brown slime boiled and belched out yellow smoke. A rotting smell hung in the air.

Elenna held her hand to her nose.

"This place stinks!" she said.

The light from Epos's wings cast sinister shadows across the cave roof. Anything could be lurking in wait for them. At the edge of the cavern a number of tunnels led in different directions. The entrances were like black mouths in the cave walls. It was uttterly silent, other than the regular dripping of water and the bubbling of the slime pools.

"This must be some sort of mine," said Elenna. "Those tunnels are manmade."

Spiros was floating in the air beside a tunnel at the far end of the underground grotto.

"She wants us to follow her," said Tom.

"I'm not sure about this," said Elenna. "How do we know which path to take?"

"We have to trust Spiros's All-Sight," Tom replied. "She wouldn't take us into danger."

Tom led the way across the cavern, hopping from rock to rock between the pools. Elenna and Epos followed, the flame bird cawing softly. They reached the spot where Spiros was waiting for them. As Tom stared into the blackness of the tunnel entrance, even he felt a tingle of doubt.

"Let me check the compass," he said, pulling it from his pocket and holding it up. Elenna came to look over his shoulder. The needle pointed to *Destiny*.

"It's settled then," said Tom. "This is the way to go."

The ghost phoenix turned and drifted into the tunnel. Tom drew his sword and followed close behind

with Elenna. Behind them came
Epos, lighting the way with her
flaming feathers.

The tunnel twisted and turned,
and Tom could tell there was a
slight downwards slope to the cave
floor. They were heading deeper
underground, further away from
the land he knew. But the Beasts
showed no fear, and Tom forced
his own heartbeat to slow.

Elenna put her hand on his arm.
"Tom," she hissed. "Look, there's
a light!"

Spiros turned and cawed softly
to urge them on. Elenna was right.
As well as the glow from Epos's
feathers, there was another source
of light in front of them. They
pressed on, and soon Tom saw a
torch hanging on the tunnel wall.

The lights sent flickering shadows across the passage.

Suddenly, there was a noise from up ahead – a high-pitched squeaking and the sound of something scraping along rock. Tom froze. He thought he could make out the scratching of claws.

"What is it?" asked Elenna.

Before Tom could answer, a rat scurried along the tunnel floor. He breathed a sigh of relief. "If that's the worst we have to deal with, I'll be happy."

There were more rats the further they went, and the stench in the air grew worse. The Beasts didn't seem to notice, but to Tom it was overwhelming. He tried not to breathe through his nose, but even then he could taste the tang of rotting flesh.

"Was that a voice?" Elenna said.

Tom cupped a hand to his ear. A faint cry sounded through the stillness. "It's my Aunt Maria!" he said. "Come on!"

CHAPTER FOUR

RESCUE!

Tom charged along the tunnel, past Spiros. He could hear Elenna's footsteps close behind him. All the time, the voices were getting louder. He ignored the foul stench in the air and the rats that scurried out of his way.

Rounding a corner, he reached a huge wooden door. Massive bronze hinges attached it to the bare rock of

the tunnel. He tried to push it open,
but it was locked from the inside.

"Help us!" came a voice.

It was Uncle Henry!

Tom threw himself at the door, but
the lock held.

"Can't you use your magical
strength?" said Elenna.

Tom rammed the door again with
his shoulder. Nothing happened.

"It must be enchanted with Malvel's
magic!" he said. "Stand back."

Tom put down his shield and
gripped the hilt of his sword in both
hands, lifting it over his head. Then,
with all the power he could muster,
he brought the blade down towards
the middle of the door. The wood
split open and one of the hinges
broke away. The sound of the impact
echoed through the tunnel. Epos

screeched with surprise.

Beyond the smashed doorway was
an enormous chamber. The walls rose
up in sheer slopes. Dangling high
above the stony ground, with coils of
rope wrapped around their middles,
were Uncle Henry and Aunt Maria.

The thick rope stretched high into the cavern above, attached somewhere out of sight. Tom's aunt and uncle squirmed when they saw him, setting the ropes creaking.

"Tom! Thank goodness!" said Aunt Maria. "Help us down!"

Tom quickly scanned the walls of the cavern, but they were completely sheer, and slick with water and moss. There wasn't a handhold in sight.

"Don't panic!" he said. "I'll think of something."

Perhaps Epos could burn through the ropes... No, that was a foolish idea. His aunt and uncle would plunge to their deaths. What they needed was something to land on. Something soft...like phoenix feathers...

"Epos!" said Tom. But the flame

bird seemed to read his mind – she was already taking to the air, lighting the upper reaches of the cavern. She let out an echoing squawk as she swooped down beneath his aunt and uncle and hovered there, so their feet brushed against her feathers.

"She's supporting them," said Elenna. "Can you use your sword to cut the ropes?"

"How?" said Tom. "I can't fly up there!"

"Throw it," said Elenna.

"What if I miss?" he said. "I might injure someone."

"We trust you," shouted Uncle Henry. "We know you won't let us down."

His uncle's words fired Tom with courage. He took careful aim, then hurled his sword through the air.

It spun in dizzying arcs across the cavern, the blade whistling, and sliced smoothly through both ropes. Tom's aunt and uncle tumbled safely onto Epos's cushioned feathers. The sword clattered onto the cavern floor.

"Well done!" shouted Elenna.

Tom rushed over to where the flame bird had landed. "I'm so happy I found you," he said, hugging his aunt and uncle tightly. "I thought I might never—"

"Shush, nephew," said Uncle Henry. "We knew you'd come. Malvel can't stand in the way of courage like yours." He turned to Elenna. "And Tom's lucky to have a companion like you."

"Thank you," Elenna said. She gave a mischievous smile. "I'm just the brains of the team!"

"She's not bad with a bow and arrow, either," said Tom, laughing. Elenna blushed. "And we wouldn't even be here without Epos."

Uncle Henry stared at the Beast. "I...I've never seen a..."

"She's a flame bird," said Tom. "A good Beast. There's nothing to fear."

Epos ruffled her feathers and cawed.

"Incredible," said Tom's uncle. "Well, thanks to all of you."

Tom's heart felt light with joy. His aunt and uncle were free, and Malvel was overcome...

Then the sound of slow clapping emerged from the gloom on the other side of the chamber.

Tom turned. "Who's there?" he said.

"Well done!" said Sethrina, stepping into the light of the cavern. Beside her lumbered Nawdren, her beak drooling thick saliva and her black talons scraping the cave floor. Epos rose to her feet and screeched in alarm.

Tom's hand darted to his hip, but his scabbard was empty.

Sethrina bent down and picked up something from the ground. "Looking for this?" she sneered, holding up Tom's sword.

"Give that back!" said Tom. "Let's make this a fair fight."

Sethrina's laughter filled the echoing space. "What makes you think I want a fair fight? My brother told me how stupid you were. Poor, brave, stupid Tom. Didn't you realise this was a trap?"

"Oh no!" said Aunt Maria.

"Drop the sword!" shouted Elenna. Tom turned to see that she'd strung her bow and was pointing an arrow at Sethrina. Nawdren gave an angry roar, filling the air with a heavy green mist. Tom moved to shield his aunt and uncle.

Elenna fired the arrow. It sped towards Sethrina, but with a deft flick of her wrist, the girl chopped the shaft in half.

"It'll take more than your pins to stop me," she mocked. "I've got Malvel's magic on my side."

Tom felt for the fragment of horseshoe on his shield. Ever since he'd freed Tagus, it had given him the ability to move at super-speed. He'd need that now.

"I've got some tricks of my own," he said. He shot forwards, and before Sethrina could draw breath, he slammed into her. Tom's sword fell from her hands.

Sethrina drew her own sword and leaped towards him, swinging her blade. Tom rolled beneath the attack

and plucked his sword from the
ground. He turned to face her.

"Now the odds are even," he said.
"Let's find out how good you
really are."

CHAPTER FIVE

THE FINAL FIGHT

Sethrina lowered her weapon and arched one black eyebrow.

"Don't you dare to fight me?" asked Tom.

Sethrina smiled and sheathed her sword. "Why should I duel with you?" she said. "I have a Beast for that. Nawdren!"

At her command the black phoenix stepped forwards. Spiros, who had been resting near the door of the cavern, let out a cry of despair. Epos screeched and moved towards Tom. He held up his hand to tell the flame bird to stop, then raised his sword. This was his battle.

Nawdren spread her wings, which spanned half the cavern, and leaped into the air, her talons outstretched. Tom pushed his aunt and uncle aside, and Nawdren slammed into the ground a shield's width from where they had been standing. The Beast smashed Tom from his feet with one of her wings, sending him flying to the edge of the cave.

Tom dizzily hauled himself up. To his horror he saw Nawdren rearing to her full height above his aunt and uncle. Her black beak looked as sharp as an axe.

"No!" he shouted.

Suddenly, in a flash of red, Epos descended onto Nawdren's back. High-pitched screeches pierced the cavern, and black and red feathers fluttered in the air.

"Uncle Henry," Tom yelled, "you have to get out of here!"

Nawdren threw Epos off her back, and the flame bird landed in a heavy heap by the cave wall. Then the black phoenix turned to attack Tom's uncle again. Tom swung his sword at the evil Beast. The blade rebounded off Nawdren's beak with a sound like a blacksmith's hammer, and sent Nawdren reeling backwards.

Tom's uncle and aunt darted towards the broken doorway.

"They're getting away!" shouted Sethrina.

Nawdren turned her massive head and bounded across the cavern after them. Tom threw a desperate glance at Epos. She was moving, but only a little. There was nothing Tom could do.

Suddenly, an arrow buried itself in Nawdren's chest feathers. Elenna! The Beast staggered. Tom's friend unleashed another shaft, which thudded next to the first. "Get back, slave of Malvel!" she cried.

Nawdren's howl of pain filled the dank air. Uncle Henry and Aunt Maria slipped through the doorway. The evil Beast bent her head to her chest and snapped the arrows away, flinging them to the cavern floor. Her eyes glowed silver with anger. Elenna fired another arrow, but Nawdren batted it away with her wing. Then she charged at Elenna.

Tom dashed to help. He swung his sword and felt it slice into Nawdren's wing. The Beast screeched again and rose off the ground. She hovered, flapping one wing frantically, the injured one half-folded into her side.

Spiros was suddenly beside her, darting at the wound.

"What's she doing?" asked Elenna. "She can't help – she's just a ghost!"

Spiros wheeled away, then dived again, letting out a desperate wail. Epos sent a cry from the cavern floor.

"She's trying to attack the wound," said Tom.

"Finish the boy!" shouted Sethrina. "Malvel wants him dead."

Nawdren twisted away from Spiros and swooped down, her talons whistling through the air. Tom lifted his shield and felt the weight of the bird crash into the wood. He was knocked to the ground as the black phoenix retreated for another attack.

"Your shield!" cried Elenna.

Tom clambered up and looked at

his shield. It was gouged where a talon had torn into the wood. This Beast was more powerful than any he had faced before.

"Your magic is no match for Malvel's!" laughed Sethrina.

Tom gripped his shield tighter and called upon the power of his golden chainmail. His chest swelled with courage. But he knew he couldn't defeat Nawdren here on the cave floor. He needed a plan. *I have to get into the air*, he thought.

The evil phoenix dived again. Tom ducked underneath her stabbing beak, then rolled between her talons, his nostrils filling with the stink of rotting feathers. There, in front of him, was Epos. Tom sprinted towards the flame bird and leaped onto her back. She immediately extended her flaming wings and flew up.

Nawdren soared after them as Tom was carried to the upper reaches of the cavern. He clutched Epos's feathers tightly as the flame bird twisted to avoid Nawdren's talons.

I must get above her! he thought. Epos seemed to understand and flapped her wings harder to rise above the evil Beast. Tom saw his chance – and leaped off Epos's back. For a moment he was weightless, then he crashed onto Nawdren's wing. His fingers struggled to grip the slimy feathers. He stabbed with his sword and pierced the wing again. Nawdren convulsed and Tom was thrown through the air. The cave floor rushed towards him, but the magic eagle's feather in his shield slowed his fall. He hit the ground hard, jolting his knees.

Nawdren squawked and drops of her black blood splashed onto the cavern floor. Sethrina's laugh pierced the cave.

"If you kill her," she said, "Spiros will never have her body back!"

As Nawdren hovered, Spiros bravely flew at her again, darting towards the injured wing. Nawdren twisted in the air, not letting the ghost draw near. Finally Tom understood.

"Elenna," Tom shouted. "Spiros is trying to reclaim her body. She needs to get in through the wounds."

"No!" said Sethrina. "You're wrong!" But Tom could hear panic in her voice. "Ignore her!" he said. "We have to keep attacking. It's the only way!"

CHAPTER SIX

THE RETURN OF SPIROS

Elenna unleashed an arrow towards Nawdren. It fell short – the Beast was too high.

Sethrina burst out laughing. "You've only got three arrows left!" she cried.

"Elenna, use Epos!" said Tom.

His friend dashed towards the flame bird. A frown creased Sethrina's pale forehead. She dived towards Elenna, swinging her sword. Tom hurled his shield and it spun through the air to catch Sethrina on the temple. She sprawled on the ground, out cold.

Now it was only the evil Beast they faced. Elenna climbed onto Epos's back.

"You need to distract Nawdren!" said Tom.

"But how will you get up there?" asked Elenna.

"Leave that to me," he replied. "Wait for my signal."

Epos sprang into the air, lighting the gloom with her wings. Nawdren swooped down to attack, and Tom's heart almost stopped. It looked as though Epos would be torn to pieces by the black phoenix's talons. But at the very last moment, the flame bird dodged to one side and rose above Nawdren. The evil Beast looped up to attack a second time.

"Now!" shouted Tom.

Elenna bravely let go of Epos's feathers and placed the first of her last three arrows to the bow's string. One after the other, she fired all three at the approaching phoenix. They whistled through the air and thudded into the Beast's feathers. Nawdren let out a loud screech.

Tom took a deep breath. *This is my only chance*, he thought.

Using his magical speed, he ran at the cavern wall, then leaped into the air. He took one, two, three, four massive strides, climbing the rock, then pushed himself off. At the same moment he twisted in the air and threw out his arms. He had no shield to stop him falling now. His hands closed around the frayed end of the rope dangling in the centre of the cavern.

With his heart pounding, he scrambled up the rope, hand over hand, until his arms burned.

Nawdren was still keening in pain as Tom climbed below her. He tugged his sword from its sheath and lunged at the black phoenix. The blade cut a long gash at the base of her wing. Her cries pierced the air as hot ash and black blood sprayed across the cave.

Tom couldn't hold on any longer and let go of the rope, tumbling downwards.

But instead of landing on hard rock, he bounced into something soft and warm. He opened his eyes to see Epos's feathers. Elenna sat astride her neck. The good Beast must have swooped down to save him.

"Thanks!" said Tom breathlessly.

He and Elenna jumped off as Epos landed. Above, Nawdren was frantically flapping her one good wing in a desperate attempt to stay aloft. The other hung limply, only half-attached to her body. Despite the battle, Tom almost felt sorry for the Beast.

"Look," whispered Elenna. "Spiros!"

The ghost phoenix swept through the cave towards the injured Beast. The green light from her eyes faded and her diamond talons dimmed to grey. As she approached Nawdren, her body seemed to become more transparent, like a wisp of cloud stretched in the wind. Then she wrapped itself around Nawdren's body and was suddenly gone. The ash stopped falling.

As Spiros poured herself into the wound in the evil phoenix's wing, Nawdren's cries became weaker and

she sank through the air. Tom
watched as she came to rest on the
cavern floor. Her black, slimy body
was completely still.

"Oh no!" said Elenna. "What have
we done?"

Tom rushed forwards. He sank to
his knees beside the huge body of the
dead bird.

But a soft cawing made him look up. The black feathers on the motionless head were glowing, first brown, then red. The colour spread across the feathers on the phoenix's back and then along its wings. Soon they were as bright as rubies, and Tom had to shield his eyes and step back. Elenna stood beside him, mouth open. The Beast lifted its head and leaped onto its jewelled talons. Finally, its eyes opened, shedding emerald light across the cavern. Nawdren had been transformed!

With a whoosh, the phoenix shot out her wings. Her injuries had magically healed. She lifted herself into the air above them, scattering dappled light into the darkness.

"It's Spiros!" said Elenna, with tears of joy in her eyes.

Epos cawed with delight and
spiralled upwards into the cavern,
adding her own light to that of her
fellow phoenix.

Tom caught sight of his aunt
and uncle at the doorway of the
chamber, gazing up. "It's safe!" he
called to them.

They walked hesitantly into the room, hand in hand, transfixed by the incredible new Beast. The magnificent phoenix swept over to Tom and Elenna and lowered her head. Tom stroked her beautiful golden beak, and she cawed softly.

"Nawdren?" said a weak voice. Tom spun round to see Sethrina sitting up and rubbing her head.

"Nawdren's gone," he said coldly.

"And Spiros has her body back!" added Elenna.

Horror contorted Sethrina's features. "It can't be!" she said. "Malvel's magic is too powerful." She reached for her sword, but Tom was too quick. He knocked it from her hand, and stood with the point of his blade at her neck.

"Good magic always overpowers evil," he said.

"This time, perhaps," spat Sethrina. "But I'm not afraid to die."

Tom looked into her dark eyes. Her hatred shone out. "I don't want to kill people," he said. "That's what makes us different."

Sethrina's mouth twisted in anger. "That's what makes you weak," she said.

"How can we get out?" said Elenna, ignoring the other girl's taunts and turning to Tom. "I don't fancy swimming through the icy water."

"She must know," said Tom's aunt, pointing at Sethrina. "She brought us here."

Sethrina lifted her chin in defiance. "Why should I tell you?" she sneered. "You'll have me locked in King Hugo's dungeon by nightfall."

Tom looked at Elenna, raising his

eyebrows. They needed Sethrina, and she knew it.

Elenna nodded. "Tell us how to get out of this place, and you can go free."

"Just like that?" said Sethrina, her voice tinged with suspicion.

"Yes," said Tom, "but you must promise never to return to Avantia again."

Sethrina frowned, then sank back, defeated. "Very well," she said.

Elenna gathered her arrows from the cavern floor and put one of them back in her bow, aiming its sharp point at Sethrina.

"Show us the way out," she said.

CHAPTER SEVEN

FAREWELL TO THE PHOENIX

Sethrina climbed to her feet and walked to the far side of the cavern. Tom, Elenna, Uncle Henry and Aunt Maria followed. Spiros and Epos hopped behind. It looked as though they were all heading towards a solid wall, but Sethrina stopped in front of it.

"Where now?" asked Tom.

Sethrina placed her hand on the slick rock and pushed. "Is no one going to help me, then?" she asked.

Tom came forwards and leaned his shoulder into the wall. It wasn't rock, he realised – just wood disguised to look like rock. He pushed again. A low grating sound echoed in the

vast space before a crack as tall as four men appeared in the cavern wall, casting a shaft of light into the dim cave. A secret door! With the help of his magical strength, it swung open. A blast of stale air filled his nostrils.

Beyond was a tunnel, roughly hewn into the bare rock. The passage was tall and narrow, but Spiros tucked her wings into her side and squeezed through.

They reached the bottom of a spiral staircase cut into the rock. Tom looked up. Above, through the heart of the coiling steps, he could see a pale circle of greenish light.

"We're almost there," he said.

"Perhaps it's a trap," said Elenna.

Tom's aunt and uncle shared a look of uncertainty.

"I'll go first," said Tom. "Epos and Spiros can fly up the middle. They'll alert us to any dangers."

As soon as they were all on the steps, the two birds took to the air and soared past them. Moments later, their caws of joy drifted back down.

"It's safe," Tom said.

Suddenly he felt a shove on his back and he tripped onto the steps. Sethrina darted up past him. When she stood on the final curve of the staircase, she looked back with a grin.

"Farewell, fools!" she shouted. "We'll meet again!"

Elenna set off after her, but Tom held her back.

"Leave her," he said. "We promised her freedom anyway."

Sethrina raced up the last few steps and was gone.

At the summit of the staircase a
green glow filled the tunnel, and
soon Tom could see why. Chinks of
daylight shone through a curtain
of leaves. Tom pushed them aside
and stepped out among trees. He
found himself standing on a ledge
beneath an outcrop of rock. A river
flowed like a silver ribbon through a
lush green valley below. Far off, the
blue sea twinkled in the sunlight. He
could see Sethrina, a distant speck,
running towards the valley.

"We must be in the northern mountains," said Tom. "We're safe again." He felt a hand on his shoulder and turned to see Uncle Henry looking down at him with pride in his eyes.

"What you did was very brave," he said.

Tom's aunt nodded in agreement. "Without you, we would have died," she added.

"It's time for you to go home to Errinel," Tom said.

"How?" asked Aunt Maria. "It must be several days' walk from here. We're not as young as we used to be, you know!"

Tom laughed. "Epos will give you a ride."

The great Beast squawked as though she understood.

Uncle Henry climbed onto Epos's back, then helped Aunt Maria to scramble up.

"What about you? Aren't you coming with us?" he asked.

Tom looked at Elenna and Spiros. "No. While Malvel is still free to wreak havoc, my job isn't done. We have to go back to Storm and Silver. There'll be more Beast Quests to come."

Tom's uncle nodded in understanding. "Be careful, both of you. And good luck!"

Epos took a few steps to the end of the ledge. She opened her massive wings and leaped off, soaring over the valley below. Tom watched the majestic Beast disappear into the distance. Uncle Henry and Aunt Maria would be back in Errinel by nightfall.

Tom turned to Spiros. "Time for you to go home, too," he said, patting the phoenix's wing.

Spiros dipped her golden beak in a bow of thanks, then ruffled her ruby feathers. She unfolded her wings, which gleamed in the sun and cast a shadow over Tom's head. He held his breath. Then the phoenix sprang into

the air, giving out a huge squawk
that carried across the empty sky.

"Oh, Tom, she's amazing!" gasped
Elenna.

"And now she's back where she
belongs," said Tom. "Guarding the
skies of Avantia. We've rescued my
aunt and uncle – but we've helped
Spiros, too. This has turned out to
be a bigger Quest than I'd ever
imagined."

Spiros swooped past them a final
time, then glided towards the horizon.

"Tom! Look!" cried Elenna,
twisting round.

Tom turned and gasped in surprise.
There, silhouetted on the slope above
them, were four huge shapes: Ferno
the fire dragon, his mouth glowing
with flame; Arcta the mountain
giant, grinning broadly and revealing

181

his brown teeth; Tagus the horse-
man, stamping the ground with his
enormous hooves; and Nanook the
snow monster, hammering her
white-furred chest with her palms.
Tom glanced back towards the sea,
and saw a flash of rainbow colours as
Sepron the sea serpent broke the

waves. He felt his shield vibrate on his arm. Their friends had gathered to congratulate them on completion of their latest Quest.

"These are the best friends I could have," Tom said, laughing and waving at the Beasts. "After you, Elenna!"

"You'll never be alone on your Quests," she said.

Tom stared out across Avantia, his home. It was safe again – for now.

"Let's go and find Storm and Silver," he said, setting off down the slope. There would be more difficult Quests to come, but whatever lay ahead of him, Tom knew he would do his best – for his friends and for Avantia.

JOIN TOM ON HIS NEXT BEAST QUEST SOON!

THE DARK REALM

Can Tom free the good
Beasts from the
Dark Realm?

Win an exclusive
Beast Quest T-shirt and goody bag!

Tom has battled many fearsome Beasts and we want to know which one is your favourite! Send us a drawing or painting of your favourite Beast and tell us in 30 words why you think it's the best.

Each month we will select **three** winners to receive a Beast Quest T-shirt and goody bag!

Send your entry on a postcard to
BEAST QUEST COMPETITION
Orchard Books, 338 Euston Road, London NW1 3BH.

Australian readers should email:
childrens.books@hachette.com.au

New Zealand readers should write to:
Beast Quest Competition, PO Box 3255, Shortland St,
Auckland 1140, NZ or email: childrensbooks@hachette.co.nz

**Don't forget to include your name and address.
Only one entry per child.**

Good luck!

Join the Quest,
Join the Tribe

www.beastquest.co.uk

Have you checked out the Beast Quest website?
It's the place to go for games, downloads, activities,
sneak previews and lots of fun!

You can read all about your favourite Beasts, download free screensavers and desktop wallpapers for
your computer, and even challenge your friends
to a Beast Tournament.

Sign up to the newsletter at www.beastquest.co.uk
to receive exclusive extra content and the opportunity to enter special members-only competitions.
We'll send you up-to-date info on all the Beast
Quest books, including the next exciting series
which features six brand-new Beasts!

Get 30% off all Beast Quest Books at www.beastquest.co.uk
Enter the code BEAST at the checkout.

All books priced at £4.99.
Special bumper editions priced at £5.99.

Orchard Books are available from all good bookshops, or can
be ordered from our website: www.orchardbooks.co.uk,
or telephone 01235 827702, or fax 01235 8227703.